WONDER WOMAN
TALES OF
PARADISE ISLAND

JET-POWERED JUSTICE

BY
MICHAEL DAHL

ILLUSTRATED BY
OMAR LOZANO

WONDER WOMAN CREATED BY
WILLIAM MOULTON MARSTON

STONE ARCH BOOKS
a capstone imprint

Published by Stone Arch Books in 2018
A Capstone Imprint
1710 Roe Crest Drive
North Mankato, Minnesota 56003
www.mycapstone.com

STAR40369

Library of Congress Cataloging-in-Publication Data is available
on the Library of Congress website.
ISBN: 978-1-5158-3023-8 (library binding)
ISBN: 978-1-5158-3032-0 (paperback)
ISBN: 978-1-5158-3028-3 (eBook PDF)

Summary: The appearance of a giant, bronze soldier in
Gateway City pits Wonder Woman against Ares and his plan
to create global chaos.

Editor: Christopher Harbo
Designer: Brann Garvey

Printed in the United States of America.
PA021

TABLE OF CONTENTS

INTRODUCTION...4

CHAPTER 1
GIANT JAM...7

CHAPTER 2
MAN OF METAL...14

CHAPTER 3
ANGRY ARES...19

CHAPTER 4
BRONZE BATTLE...24

CHAPTER 5
JET OF JUSTICE...28

BEHOLD, PARADISE ISLAND!

INVISIBLE JET

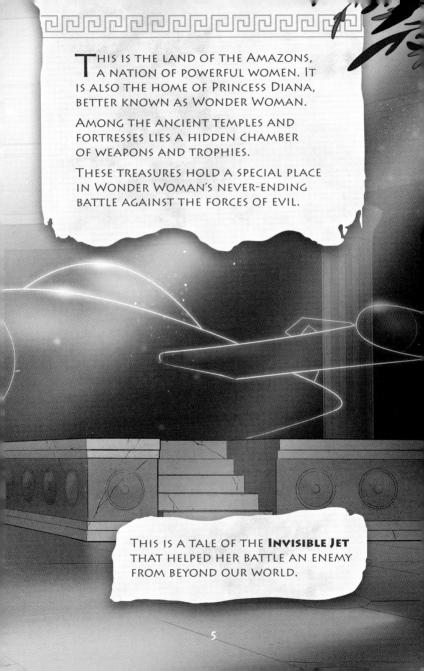

This is the land of the Amazons, a nation of powerful women. It is also the home of Princess Diana, better known as Wonder Woman.

Among the ancient temples and fortresses lies a hidden chamber of weapons and trophies.

These treasures hold a special place in Wonder Woman's never-ending battle against the forces of evil.

This is a tale of the **Invisible Jet** that helped her battle an enemy from beyond our world.

CHAPTER 1

##

On a sunny afternoon, Wonder Woman
enjoys a ride with her friend, Steve Trevor.
He is driving his sports car across the bridge
that leads to Gateway City.

Wonder Woman closes her eyes and leans her
head back.

The sun feels so good and warm, she thinks.
It's turning out to be a beautiful day!

HONNNNK!
HONNNNK!

The car suddenly stops. Wonder Woman's eyes snap open.

"Steve, what's wrong?" the hero asks.

Steve stares out the window with a frown.

"A giant traffic jam!" he says.

All the traffic lanes leading into the city are blocked. Cars, trucks, buses, and motorcycles are at a standstill.

Angry people honk their horns. A few drivers step out of their cars, looking toward the city.

Steve says, "I wonder how long it will—"

"Steve, look!" says Wonder Woman, cutting him off. She steps out of the sports car and looks toward the city.

AAAAAIIIIIIIEEEEEEE!

Several people on the bridge begin to scream. Off in the distance, a huge shadowy figure towers above the buildings.

"A giant!" says Wonder Woman.

"It can't be the villain Giganta," Steve says, shaking his head. "You captured her recently."

"I have to go," says Wonder Woman. She walks toward the edge of the bridge and thinks a silent command.

Come to me, she says in her mind.

VROOOOSSHHH!

Wonder Woman's Invisible Jet swoops out of the sky.

CHAPTER 2

MAN OF METAL

The Invisible Jet dives toward the bridge.

As it zooms closer, Wonder Woman leaps into the air. She flies over the parked cars and trucks.

Just as the jet dips below the bridge deck, Wonder Woman lands in the open cockpit.

ZHOOOOOOMMMM!

Wonder Woman steers the jet toward Gateway City.

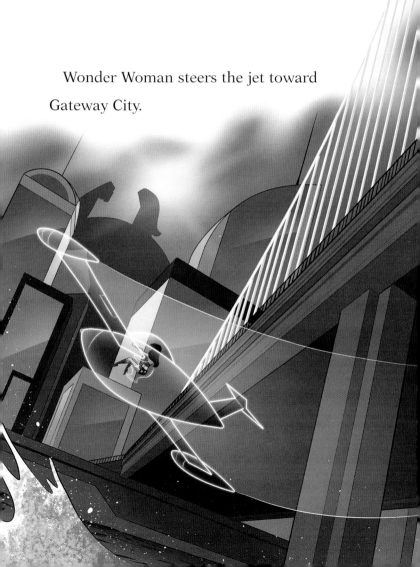

"I need a better look at that giant," Wonder Woman says to herself.

Zooming over the city's buildings, the Amazon Princess sees the towering menace up close.

It is a gigantic warrior made of bronze.

The huge man lifts a massive bronze sword. Sunlight flashes off the blade. He slashes the sword toward the swooping jet.

SWIIISSSHHH!

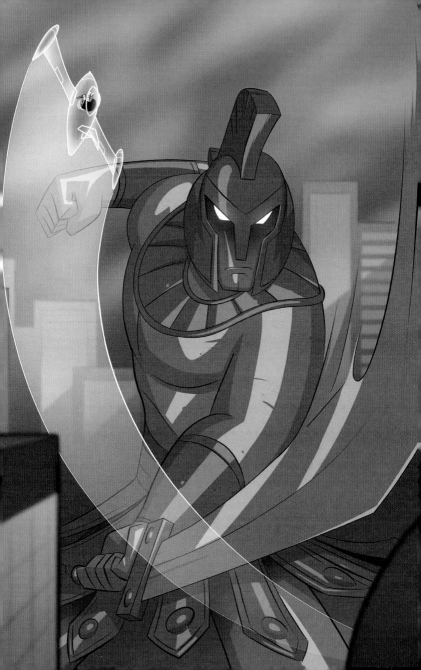

Wonder Woman guides the Invisible Jet swiftly past the deadly weapon.

WHOOOOSHHHHH!

This creature doesn't look man-made, thinks the hero. *Someone from Olympus must be behind this.*

CHAPTER 3

ANGRY ARES

An angry, dark cloud appears above the bronze giant.

A titanic helmet with glowing eyes rises from the swirling mist.

"Ares!" shouts Wonder Woman.

The God of War looks down at the city.

"I see you've met Talos, my newest weapon," says Ares.

"Why have you left Olympus?" asks the Amazon warrior.

"Humans are stupid creatures," the villain says. "They will think Talos was sent from another country. He will start another war!"

HA! HA! HA! HA! HA!

The God of War laughs. Bright lightning
crashes from the swirling cloud.

"Soon the humans will call the military to
help them," says Ares. "With more fighting and
destruction, my power will grow stronger."

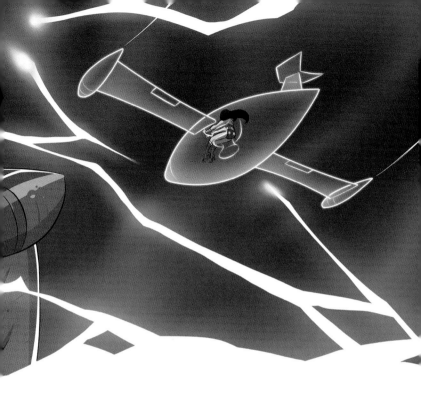

"Not if I can help it!" shouts the Amazon.

Ares laughs again and disappears.

Wonder Woman aims her jet toward the bronze giant.

CHAPTER 4

BRONZE BATTLE

Talos' massive feet crush empty police cars on the streets below.

As Wonder Woman closes in on the giant, she leaps out of the jet.

"This calls for hand-to-hand combat," the Amazon warrior says.

Wonder Woman grabs her golden lasso. She twirls the rope and then tosses it at the giant.

The lasso captures Talos' fist as he swipes at a nearby news helicopter. The fist pulls the lasso and Wonder Woman along with it.

"My lasso's not working!" says Wonder Woman. "It has no effect on him because he's made of metal. He's not human."

Wonder Woman hears the cries of people in the streets.

I need more power! she thinks.

CHAPTER 5

JET OF JUSTICE

Wonder Woman jumps back into her Invisible Jet. She buzzes round and round the rampaging robot.

"Perhaps I could zoom in a circle and wrap him up in a cable," she says to herself.

Talos marches along a busy street.

But if Talos falls, he could harm the citizens and police, Wonder Woman thinks.

The Amazon warrior feels warmth on her face. Sunlight passes through the windshield of the Invisible Jet

"Heat!" she says to herself. "Of course!"

Wonder Woman zooms even closer to the bronze menace.

The giant's sword strikes at her again.

Wonder Woman punches a button. Flames flare from the Invisible Jet's engines.

The high heat melts the giant's bronze blade.

"You're just metal, Talos!" shouts Wonder
Woman. "And my jet can withstand super
hot temperatures."

The swift jet sweeps past Talos' bronze helmet. The headgear begins to melt. Liquid metal covers the giant's face and blinds him.

Again and again, the jet skims across the giant's body. Talos melts and sinks slowly, and safely, into the street.

"I guess Talos couldn't handle the heat!" says Wonder Woman.

Ares' voice booms out from the dark cloud above the city.

"You won this time, Amazon," he says. "But I'll be back!"

The angry cloud dissolves in the sunlight as the Invisible Jet soars back to the busy bridge.

GLOSSARY

bronze (BRAHNZ)—a metal made of copper and tin; bronze has a gold-brown color

citizen (SI-tuh-zuhn)—a member of a country or state who has the right to live there

cockpit (KOK-pit)—the area in the front of a plane where the pilot sits

combat (KOM-bat)—fighting between people or armies

headgear (HED-geer)—a covering for the head, such as a hat or helmet

menace (MEN-iss)—someone who is a threat or danger to others

military (MIL-uh-ter-ee)—the armed forces of a state or country

Olympus (oh-LIM-pus)—the home of the gods in Greek mythology

villain (VIL-uhn)—a wicked, evil, or bad person who is often a character in a story

DISCUSS

1. Wonder Woman uses her mind to call her Invisible Jet. Imagine if you could control things with your mind. What would you control and why?

2. How do the illustrations for this story get across the idea that Wonder Woman's jet is invisible? How else could the art show something that can't be seen?

3. Wonder Woman uses heat to melt the metal giant. What other ways could she have used to defeat it?

WRITE

1. Imagine if you could create a giant robot like Talos. What would your robot be and what would you do with it? Write a short story about your robot's adventures.

2. Ares comes from Olympus, the mountain home of the Greek gods. Write a paragraph describing what you think Olympus looks like and draw a picture of it.

3. Wonder Woman defeats Ares at the end of the story. But the God of War says he'll be back. Write a short story where Ares returns and Wonder Woman must face him again.

AUTHOR

Michael Dahl is the prolific author of more than 200 books for children and young adults, including *Bedtime for Batman*, *Be A Star, Wonder Woman!*, and *Sweet Dreams, Supergirl.* He has won the AEP Distinguished Achievement Award three times for his nonfiction, a Teachers' Choice Award from *Learning* magazine, and a Seal of Excellence from the Creative Child Awards. He is also the author of the Batman Tales of the Batcave and Superman Tales of the Fortress of Solitude series. Dahl currently lives in Minneapolis, Minnesota.

ILLUSTRATOR

Omar Lozano lives in Monterrey, Mexico. He has always been crazy for illustration and is constantly on the lookout for awesome things to draw. In his free time, he watches lots of movies, reads fantasy and sci-fi books, and draws! Omar has worked for Marvel, DC, IDW, Capstone, and several other publishing companies.